The Nightingale

Ilustrações © Priscila Wu

© Editora do Brasil S.A., 2024
Todos os direitos reservados

Direção-geral	Paulo Serino de Souza
Direção editorial	Felipe Ramos Poletti
Gerência editorial de produção e design	Ulisses Pires
Supervisão editorial	Carla Felix Lopes e Diego da Mata
Edição	Camile Mendrot | Ab Aeterno
Assistência editorial	Marcos Vasconcelos e Pedro Andrade Bezerra; Enrico Payão | Ab Aeterno
Auxílio editorial	Natalia Soeda
Supervisão de arte	Abdonildo José de Lima Santos
Edição de arte e diagramação	Ana Clara Suzano | Ab Aeterno
Design gráfico	Ariane Adriele O. Costa
Supervisão de revisão	Elaine Cristina da Silva
Revisão	Natasha Greenhouse e Sarah Garnett | Ab Aeterno

1ª edição / 1ª impressão, 2024
Impresso na Hawaii Gráfica e Editora

Avenida das Nações Unidas, 12901
Torre Oeste, 20º andar
São Paulo, SP – CEP: 04578-910
Fone: +55 11 3226-0211
www.editoradobrasil.com.br

The Nightingale

TRADUÇÃO E ADAPTAÇÃO:
MARIA CAROLINA RODRIGUES
ILUSTRAÇÕES: PRISCILA WU

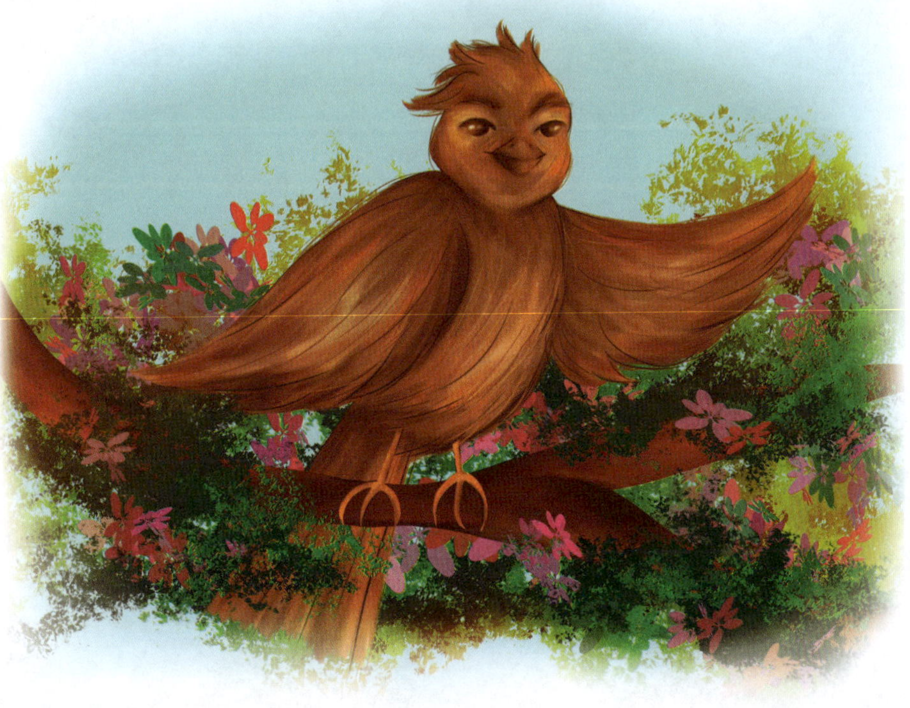

In spring, he walks in the forest to see all the flowers.

One day, he meets a nightingale. The bird sings beautiful songs. "Do you want to come live with me and sing to me?" the man asks.

The nightingale says: "Birds have to fly and be free, but I can be your friend and visit you." The man agrees, happy. It is nice to make new friends.

Spring turns to summer. Days are hot and long. The nightingale visits his new friend and sings many songs.

Summer turns to fall. The leaves are brown and the wind is cold.
The nightingale visits the man and sings at night to help his friend sleep better.

Fall turns to winter. Snow falls. The nightingale visits, this time to say goodbye.
It is time to fly home.

Winter turns to spring again and the nightingale returns.
But the man has a metal bird now.
The nightingale is sad to lose a friend.

Spring turns to summer, summer turns to fall, and fall turns to winter.

The nightingale visits his friend again.

The man is sick, and the metal bird is broken.

The man gets better and the nightingale flies home. Friends are still friends, even when far away.